CHAPTER I
East Jordan
Elementary School

The THREE BILLY GOATS GRUFF

Illustrated by
Ed Parker

Troll Associates

Troll Associates, Mahwah, N.J.

Library of Congress Catalog Card Number: 78-18068
ISBN 0-89375-121-9

Once upon a time there were three billy goats. And
the last name of all three was Gruff.

To make themselves fat, the billy goats Gruff had to go high up the side of a hill, where there was plenty of grass. But on the way up the hill, there was a bridge that crossed over a brook. And under the bridge lived a mean, ugly troll. His eyes were as big as saucers and his nose was as long as a poker.

The youngest billy goat Gruff was the first to cross over the bridge. *Trip trap, trip trap* went his feet.

"Who's that going over my bridge?" called the troll.

"It is I," answered a tiny voice. "I am the tiniest of the billy goats Gruff. I am going up the hillside, where I will make myself fat."

"And I am coming up there to gobble you up!"
roared the troll.

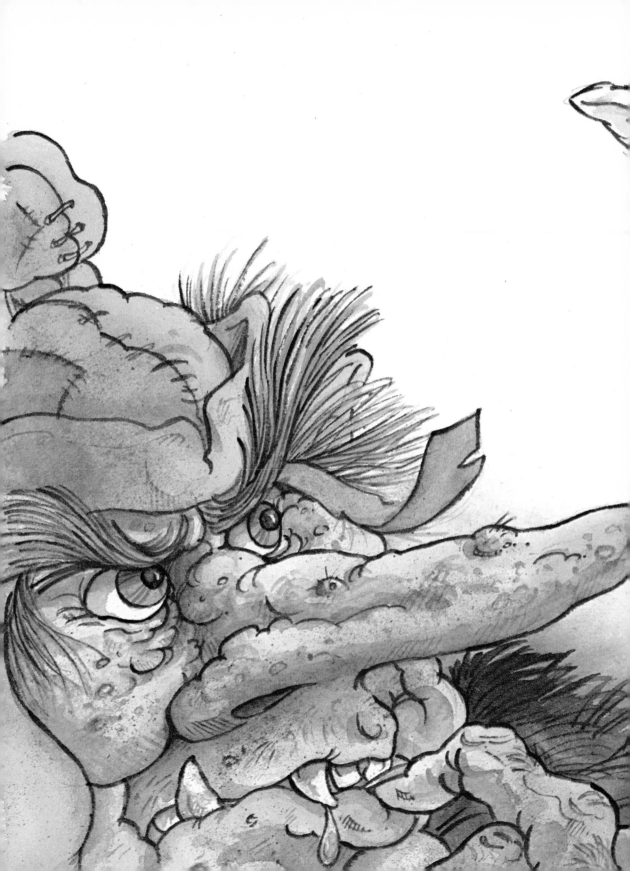

"Oh no! Don't eat *me*!" begged the little billy goat.
"I'm much too small. Why not wait a little while, until the
second billy goat Gruff comes along. After all, he is much
bigger than I."

So the troll muttered, "All right; now be off with you!"

After a little while, the second billy goat Gruff started across the bridge. *Trip trap, trip trap, trip trap* went his feet.

"Who's that tripping over my bridge?" cried the troll.

"It is I," answered a middle-sized voice. "I am the second billy goat Gruff, and I am going up the hillside, so I can make myself fat."

"Well, I'm coming up there to gobble you up!"
roared the troll.

"No, no! don't eat *me*!" cried the middle-sized billy goat. "Why not wait for the big billy goat Gruff? He'll be here soon, and he is bigger than I."

"Very well," grumbled the troll. "Now, be off with you."

Soon the biggest of the billy goats Gruff started over the bridge. *Trip trap, trip trap, trip trap, trip trap* went his feet. He was so big and heavy that the bridge began to creak and groan.

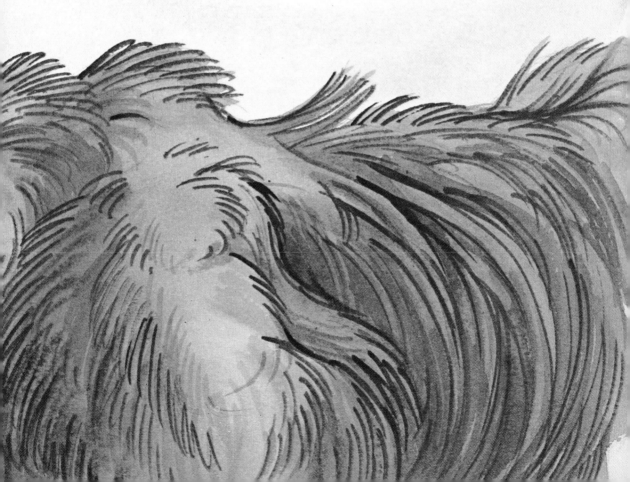

"Who's that tramping over my bridge?" roared the
troll.

"It is I, the biggest of the billy goats Gruff!" said the
big billy goat. His voice was deep and hoarse and loud.

"Then I'm coming up there to gobble you up!"
roared the troll. And the big billy goat Gruff answered:

Well come along! I've got two spears
And I'll poke your eyeballs out at your ears.
I've got besides two great big stones,
And I'll crush you to bits, body and bones.

And that's exactly what the big billy goat did. He lowered his horns and charged. He poked out the wicked troll's eyes, crunched his bones, and butted him into the brook. Then he walked over the bridge and up the hill, and he joined the other billy goats Gruff. They all grew so fat that they could hardly walk. And if the fat hasn't fallen off yet, they must still be fat!

Snip, snap, snout,
This tale's told out.

CHAPTER I
East Jordan
Elementary School